THE LIGHT *in the* WINDOW

GARY LEE VINCENT

The Light in the Window
By **Gary Lee Vincent**

Burning Bulb Publishing
P.O. Box 4721
Bridgeport, WV 26330-4721
United States of America
www.BurningBulbPublishing.com

First Edition.

Paperback Edition ISBN: 978-1-964172-60-6

Dedicated to
Julia Beall.

PART ONE

The Closed Door

One

There is a road that leaves Prescott going south and east, and after a few miles it forgets it was ever a town road and becomes something else. It climbs. It loses its shoulder. The pavement narrows and then surrenders altogether to a strip of red dirt that the rain remembers and the snow remembers and the sun, in summer, bakes to the color of old brick. Ponderosas lean in over the road on either side, tall and unhurried, and the light that falls through them onto the dirt is the kind of light that makes a man slow his truck without knowing why.

It is the sixteenth of November. Late afternoon. The sky is the color of dishwater and the wind is moving in the high boughs in a way that promises something — rain, maybe, or the first snow of the season, the kind that slips down off the Bradshaws once a year in November and reminds the country that it is, after all, a mountain.

Henry Marshall — Hank to anyone who has ever loved him — drives the road as though he has driven it a thousand times, which he has. His hands rest on the wheel the way a man's hands rest on a wheel after forty years of resting there. The truck is a 1994 Ford F-150, dark green where it is not rust, and it knows the curves the way the man knows them, which is to say, by feel, in the bones, without consulting the eyes.

In the bed of the truck are two cardboard boxes, a roll of contractor bags, and a duffel that contains three changes of clothes and a Bible he has not opened in six months and twelve days.

He is sixty-seven years old. His hair is the color of weathered cedar and his hands are the texture and he has not shaved in four days. There is a small scar above his left eyebrow that he got at twenty-two, putting up a roof in a wind he should have known better than to put up a roof in, and there is a wedding band on the third finger of his left hand that he has not been able to bring himself to take off.

His wife's name was Eleanor. She has been dead since the seventh of May.

Two

The cabin sits on three-quarters of an acre on the back side of a draw, half a mile up from where the dirt road branches. You cannot see it from the branch. You have to know it is there. Eleanor's father built it in 1962 with his own two hands and the help of a Mormon neighbor named Brother Lyman, and the two of them put up the walls in a single summer out of ponderosa logs they cut on the property. The roof is green tin. The porch faces east, toward where the sun comes up over the Mingus range. There are two rocking chairs on the porch and a porch rail Eleanor's father planed by hand, and the rail is rounded now in two places where forty years of forearms and coffee cups have worn it smooth.

Hank pulls the truck up to the porch and cuts the engine and sits a long time with his hands on the wheel.

The wind moves in the pines.

A pinecone, somewhere up the slope, lets go of its branch and falls and is heard.

He gets out. He climbs the three steps onto the porch. The brass key is on a leather fob that Eleanor stitched for him their first year of marriage, when she was learning leatherwork and he was pretending to need a key fob, and he has carried that key on that fob now for forty-one years. He puts it in the lock. The lock is stiff. He works it. It gives.

The door swings inward on six months of dust and on the smell of a house that has not been lived in, which is a smell that has nothing to do with neglect and everything to do with absence. It is the smell of a kitchen with no one cooking in it. A bedroom with no one breathing in it. A great room with the wood stove gone cold and stayed cold through two summers of high heat and into a third autumn.

Hank stands in the doorway.

He does not cry. He has not cried since the funeral, which he considers, privately and without saying it aloud to anyone, to be one of the failures of his life.

He sees, on the kitchen table, a half-finished crossword puzzle. The pencil is laid across it at an angle, the way a person lays a pencil across a puzzle when she means to come back to it after lunch. He sees Eleanor's reading glasses folded on top of the crossword. He sees the corner of a teabag, dried and shriveled now to the color and texture of an old leaf, hooked over the rim of a mug that says WORLD'S OKAYEST GRANDMA.

He had forgotten that mug.

He stands in the doorway and he looks at the mug and he thinks: She left her tea.

It is a small thing. It should not be the thing that does it. But that is how grief works. Grief does not announce itself at the funeral or at the empty side of the bed or at the closet door. Grief waits. It sits patiently in the corner of a room for six months, with its hands folded, and then one afternoon when you are not looking it gets up and walks across the floor and puts its hand on your shoulder and says, very quietly: She left her tea.

He sets down the duffel. He walks to the mantle. Above the mantle is a wooden cross that Eleanor's father carved out of a piece of oak in the same summer he built the cabin, with a chisel and a patience that the world, in the opinion of the carver, was beginning even then to lose.

Hank takes the cross down off its nail.

He turns it over.

He hangs it back on the nail with the carved face to the wall and the plain back of it facing the room.

He stands there for a moment with his hand still on the wood.

"I am sorry," he says, not loud, not to anyone in particular. "I just can't look at you right now."

Three

He works through the rest of that afternoon and into the dusk.

He brings in firewood from the lean-to on the north side of the cabin and stacks it by the stove. He does not light the stove. He opens the windows in the bedroom and the great room and lets the cold mountain air come in and pull the absence out, or some of the absence, some of it being the kind of absence that does not leave because you opened a window. He pulls the dust covers off the couch and the two leather reading chairs by the fireplace. He considers carrying Eleanor's reading glasses, still folded, into the bedroom and sitting them on the nightstand on her side, which is the side closest to the window, because she liked to wake to the first light.

He does not touch the crossword. He does not touch the mug. And after the brief consideration, he does not touch the glasses.

In the kitchen he opens the cabinets one by one and stands in front of each of them as though he is taking inventory of something, but he is not taking inventory of anything. He is looking at her handwriting on the spice jars. Cumin. Bay leaf. Cardamom. She wrote in a slanted, slightly impatient cursive that always tilted forward, leaning into the next letter the way she leaned, in life, into the next thing — into a conversation, into a piece of music, into a guest at the door.

There is a tin of flour in the back of the corner cabinet. He can see her handwriting on the lid: ELLIE'S. SEPT. He shuts the cabinet.

He sits down at the kitchen table across from the crossword puzzle and the cold tea and the glasses he has not moved, and he puts his hands flat on the wood, and he looks at his hands.

These are the hands, he thinks, that built half the cabinets in this house.

Four

It comes on dark early in November in the high country. By five-thirty the windows are already gone blue and by six they are black, and the wind that has been moving in the pines all afternoon has shifted, sometime in the last hour, into something with weight in it. A storm wind. A wind that has come up off the desert and is now climbing the mountain and getting colder as it climbs.

Hank stands at the kitchen sink and looks out the window into the dark.

He has not eaten since a gas station coffee in Wickenburg.

He thinks, *I should drive down to town. I should eat something.*

He thinks, *I am not hungry.*

He thinks, *You will be hungry by the time you sit down somewhere, and you have not eaten today, and Eleanor would have something to say about that.*

He almost smiles. The almost-smile is, by his own private accounting, the closest he has come to a smile in some weeks.

He gets his keys.

Five

The drive down off the mountain in the dark is a drive he could do in his sleep, and there was a stretch of years, when Eleanor was sick, when he very nearly did. The truck's headlights make twin yellow channels in the dust, and the channels run ahead of him into the pines and disappear, and then there are more pines, and the channels reach into them, and disappear again. He does not turn on the radio. The truck has a radio. The truck had Eleanor in the passenger seat for forty years and the radio was hers, and the radio has not been on since the first week of May.

Prescott in November, on a Tuesday evening, is a town with its hands in its pockets. The Courthouse Plaza is lit up, the big elms along the lawn already bare, the white lights strung in the branches not yet turned on for Christmas but only a week or two from being turned on. A few people are walking dogs around the square. The old courthouse sits in the middle of it all the way it has sat in the middle of it all for over a hundred years, square-shouldered, indifferent to weather.

He parks on Cortez. He walks half a block to a diner he and Eleanor used to come to after a movie, when there was a movie they wanted to see at the Elks Theater and they would make a night of it. The diner has not changed in twenty years, which is part of why he goes there. There is a hand-lettered sign in the window that says PIE TODAY: APPLE, PUMPKIN, COCONUT CREAM. There is a bell over the door, and the bell rings when he comes in, and a waitress in her late fifties looks up from a coffeepot at the back counter and her face does something complicated.

"Hank," she says.

"Hi, Marlene," he says.

Marlene comes out from behind the counter with the coffeepot still in her hand, as though she has forgotten she is holding it. She is a small woman with hair the color of a brown paper bag and a face that has been kind to a great many strangers for a great many years.

"Sit anywhere, hon," she says. Then she says, "We were so sorry. About Ellie. We sent a card."

"I got it," Hank says. "Thank you."

He sits in a booth by the window. Marlene brings him coffee without asking and stands there for a moment with the pot held a little away from her hip, the way a person stands when she wants to say something and is not sure if she should.

"She always tipped on the full check," Marlene says finally. "Even before the senior discount kicked in. I just want you to know that. We talked about her, after. The girls and me. She always tipped on the full check."

"That sounds like her," Hank says.

Marlene nods. She goes away. She comes back with a menu he will not need and sets it down anyway.

Hank orders a patty melt and a bowl of vegetable soup. He drinks his coffee black. The window beside the booth looks out on Cortez Street, and across Cortez is the lawn of the Plaza with its bare elms and its strung lights, and through the window he can see the lights of the Palace Saloon down the block on Whiskey Row, throwing yellow onto the brick of the sidewalk.

He eats slowly. He had not, until the soup, realized he was hungry.

Six

Outside, after, he stands on the sidewalk for a moment with his hands in the pockets of his coat. The wind is up. The flag in front of the courthouse is making the sound flags make in a serious wind, which is a sound like cloth being torn, very slowly, by a patient hand.

He walks the long way back to the truck, around the square. He is not in a hurry to get back to the cabin. He is not in a hurry to get anywhere. He walks past the war memorial and past the bandstand and past the place where, in the summers, the bluegrass bands play on Saturday nights, and as he comes around the south side of the Plaza he sees, on a bench under one of the bare elms, a young woman with a hiking pack at her feet and a dog on a length of clothesline.

She is feeding the dog something. Half a hamburger, it looks like. The dog is eating very politely, as though the dog has been hungry for some time and is concentrating on not seeming hungry.

The young woman is not looking at Hank. She is not looking at anyone. She is looking down at the dog and her hair has fallen forward across her face and her free hand is resting on the dog's head, between his ears, the way a person's hand rests on a dog's head when the dog is the one steady thing the person has.

He does not stop. He walks past her, on the far side of the path, and she does not look up.

He thinks, as he passes, only this: *That girl is too young to be sitting alone in the dark on a bench in November.*

He gets to his truck. He gets in. He drives north out of town, through the lights, and turns east, and the lights fall away behind him, and the dirt road begins.

It begins to rain about a mile up the road.

By the time he turns onto his own road, where the pavement has long since given up and the dirt narrows between the pines, the rain is coming down in sheets. The wipers cannot keep up with it. He has the headlights on high and even on high they pick up only the nearest twenty feet of road, the rest of it disappearing into a wall of water, and the water is coming so hard it bounces back up off the dirt in a fine red mist that rises to the level of his bumper and obscures everything beyond it.

He is driving slow. Maybe fifteen.

That is how he sees her.

Seven

She is walking on the right shoulder, which is not so much a shoulder as the place where the dirt road ends and the forest begins. She is walking with her head down against the rain, the hiking pack hunched on her back, and the dog is a half step behind her on the clothesline, limping. The dog is favoring his right hindquarter.

She does not turn around when the headlights come up behind her. She steps farther off the road, into the weeds, and keeps walking.

Hank passes her.

He drives a quarter mile up the road before he becomes aware that he has been holding his breath.

He pulls over.

He sits with the engine running and the wipers going and the rain hammering on the hood of the truck, and he stares straight ahead at the place where his headlights end, and he says aloud to nobody: "She had a dog with her."

He sits there.

The wipers slap.

He is not, by nature, a man who does things on impulse. He is a man who measures twice and cuts once, and the measuring he has done over a lifetime is part of why his cabinets, in three states, are still hanging plumb thirty and forty years after he hung them. Measuring is not a sin. Measuring is a kind of respect — for wood, for time, for the people who will live with the thing you make.

But there are nights when measuring is a sin, and a man with any sense at all knows the difference.

There is a girl walking up the mountain in the rain in the dark, he thinks, *and she has a dog, and the dog is hurt.*

He thinks, *You will not sleep tonight if you do not turn this truck around.*

He thinks, perhaps not in words, perhaps only somewhere underneath the words, in the place where a man keeps the things he does not say even to himself: *Eleanor would have already turned around.*

He turns the truck around.

The road is narrow and the rain is bad and it takes him three points to do it, the back tires sliding once in the soft red mud at the edge, and then the headlights are pointing back the way he came, and he is driving slow, slower than he came up, looking. For a long moment he thinks he has missed her. He thinks she has stepped off the road into the trees, to wait the rain out, and that he will pass her without seeing her.

Then, in the headlights, the dog. The pale shape of the dog first, low to the ground, looking up.

And behind the dog, the girl.

She has stopped walking. She is standing in the rain with her hood pushed back, the rain running off her hair, looking at the truck.

He stops the truck ten feet from her. He rolls down the window. The rain comes in.

"I'm not going to hurt you," he says, into the rain, into the headlights, into the dark. "I live half a mile up. There's a porch and a wood stove. You and the dog are welcome to ride out the storm. I'll sleep in the great room. You can have the couch and the door locks from the inside."

She looks at him for a long time.

The rain runs off her hair and off her chin and off the sleeves of her jacket.

The dog sits down on the wet road and looks up at her.

"All right," she says.

Her voice is younger than he expected, and tireder.

She walks around to the passenger side. She lifts the dog up into the cab first, with both hands, the way you lift a child, and the dog does not resist, only looks at her with the patient, suffering expression of a dog who has been wet for a long time and would like, eventually, not to be. Then she climbs in herself, the pack still on her back, and she pulls the door shut.

Hank does not look at her. He gives her that.

He puts the truck in gear.

He drives the half mile up the mountain, through the rain, without speaking, and the dog sits on the seat between them and drips quietly onto the upholstery, and somewhere up ahead, through the pines, beyond the rain, the cabin is waiting in the dark with no lamp burning in any of its windows, because nobody has lived in it since May.

That will change tonight.

PART TWO

Three Days Under One Roof

Eight

The headlights find the cabin the way headlights find a thing you have been driving toward for a long time, which is to say all at once and without ceremony. The pale logs come up out of the rain. The green tin roof. The two rocking chairs on the porch, beaded over now with water, and behind them the dark shape of the door.

Hank pulls the truck up close to the porch steps, closer than he would normally park, so that the passenger side opens almost onto the porch itself. He cuts the engine. The wipers stop in the middle of a sweep and the rain takes over the windshield immediately, sheeting down it, and the cab fills with the sound of rain on metal and the wet, even breathing of the dog between them.

He looks at her for the first time since she got in.

She is younger than he had thought from the headlights. Twenty-three, twenty-four. Her hair is dark and wet and parted in the middle and stuck flat to her temples. There is a small silver cross at the hollow of her throat on a chain so fine it is more suggestion than chain. Her jacket is a thin army-green thing meant for late summer, not for November in the high country, and the cuffs of it are dark with water all the way to the elbows.

She is looking straight ahead at the cabin.

"The porch is right there," he says. "Go on. Take the dog. The door's not locked. I'll bring your pack."

She nods once. She gets out. The dog goes with her, springing down out of the cab on three good legs and one bad one, and she catches him by the clothesline and steadies him, and the two of them go up onto the porch out of the rain. She does not turn around to watch Hank.

He hauls her pack out of the cab. It is heavier than he expected. There is a bedroll lashed to the bottom of it and a folded blue tarp lashed to the top, and the canvas is dark with rain all over. He carries it up onto the porch. He sets it down beside her.

She is standing very still under the porch eave with the dog pressed against her leg. She is shivering. She is shivering so hard that her shoulders are moving in a small continuous tremor he can see even in the bad light.

"Inside," he says.

He opens the door. He stands aside.

She goes in. The dog goes in. He shuts the door behind them.

Nine

He turns on the lamp on the side table by the leather chair, because he wants light in the room before he wants anything else, and then he turns on the kitchen light, and then the small lamp on the bookshelf, and then he stops, because three lamps is more than this cabin has had on at the same time in six months and twelve days, and he does not want to overdo it.

The girl is standing just inside the door on the rag rug, dripping. She is looking around the cabin the way a person in a strange house at night looks around a strange house at night, which is to say she is pretending not to be looking and missing nothing.

He sees her see the wood stove. The leather chairs. The fireplace. The mantle. The cross above the mantle, plain side out, the carved face turned to the wall.

Her eyes pass over the cross without lingering. He notes that. He does not know what to make of it yet.

"There's a bathroom through there," he says, pointing. "There's towels in the cabinet under the sink. The blue ones are clean. I'll start the stove. You get out of those wet things first. Anything you need that's in your pack, take it in with you."

She nods. She hesitates.

"What's the dog's name?" he says.

"Boaz," she says.

He almost smiles. The almost-smile, again. Twice in one day, after weeks of nothing.

"That's a good name," he says.

It is the first thing he has said to her that is not directions. She looks at him for a second longer than she has looked at him before. Then she crouches down and unties the clothesline from Boaz's collar, and she scratches the dog once, hard, between his ears, and she straightens up, and she takes a stuff sack out of the top of the pack, and she goes through the door he pointed to and shuts it behind her.

The dog stands on the rag rug. The dog looks at Hank.

"You and me, then," Hank says.

He goes to the stove.

Ten

There is a science to a wood stove and there is an art to it, and most men who have lived around them for long enough have stopped being able to tell which is which. Hank kneels in front of the stove on the cold flagstone hearth. He opens the door. He lays a base of crumpled newspaper from a stack of papers in the kindling box, papers that are six months and twelve days old now and going yellow at the edges, the headlines of a world that was already gone the day Eleanor died and is, by now, no kind of news at all. He lays kindling over the paper. He lays two splits of pine on top of the kindling in a cross. He strikes a match.

The fire takes the way fire takes when it has been laid by a man who knows what he is doing — slow at first, with a single flame walking sideways across the paper, and then the kindling catching, and then the pine, and then the small private roar of a fire deciding to be a fire.

He shuts the stove door. He opens the damper a quarter of the way.

He stays there on his knees on the hearth for a moment longer than the fire needs him to.

He is praying, possibly. Or he is not. He himself could not tell you which.

If it is a prayer, it is one of the wordless ones. The kind that a man kneeling in front of a fire on a stone hearth in November sends up almost in spite of himself, on behalf of a girl in his bathroom who is twenty-three or twenty-four and who has been walking up a mountain in the rain at night, and on behalf of a dog with a hurt leg who is standing on his rag rug, and on behalf of his own self, who has come to this cabin to close it up and is now lighting a fire in it for the first time in two winters because a stranger needed to come in out of the weather.

If it is a prayer, it is not addressed to anyone in particular. It is sent up the way a man sends smoke up a flue. Out, and away, and somewhere.

He gets up off his knees.

He goes into the kitchen.

Eleven

There is not much in the kitchen. He had not, when he packed, expected to be feeding anyone but himself, and even himself only for as many days as it took to put the cabin on the market. There is a loaf of bread in the truck still. There is a brick of cheddar and a pound of bacon in the cooler on the floor of the cab. There is a can of vegetable soup in the duffel.

He goes back out into the rain, head down, and brings in the cooler and the bag of groceries from the truck. The rain has, if anything, gotten harder. He stands on the porch a minute when he comes back, with the cooler still in his hand, and he looks out into the dark beyond the porch railing, where the pines are moving in the wind like something underwater.

He thinks, *This is going to turn to snow before morning.*

He goes inside.

He puts a saucepan of soup on the gas burner. He cuts two thick slices of bread. He gets the cheddar out of the cooler and cuts four slices of cheese. He butters the bread on one side and puts it butter-side-down in the cast iron skillet that Eleanor's mother bought new in 1958 and that has been on the stovetop in this cabin every day since, and the skillet is black and slick with sixty-seven years of use, and the butter takes immediately and begins to brown.

He hears the bathroom door open behind him. He does not turn around. He gives her that.

He hears her cross to where he set her pack against the wall. He hears her open it and close it. He hears her bare feet on the wood floor — bare, because her socks must have been soaked too — and he hears the small, careful sound of a woman trying to be quiet in a strange man's kitchen.

"I made grilled cheese," he says, to the skillet. "There's tomato soup. Vegetable, I mean. There's vegetable soup. Sit down anywhere."

He hears her sit down at the table.

He plates up. Two grilled cheese, two bowls of soup. He carries them over without looking at her directly. He sets hers down. He sits down across from her.

She is wearing dry clothes from her pack. Gray sweatpants and a flannel shirt that is too big for her, the cuffs rolled twice, and her wet hair has been towel-dried and is now sticking up at the back in a small dark cowlick that she is unaware of and that, for some reason, makes Hank's chest tighten.

She has not touched the food. She is looking at the table.

The crossword puzzle is still there, between them. The pencil. The reading glasses. The mug.

She looks at the crossword. She does not say anything about it.

"Eat," he says. "Before it gets cold."

She eats. She eats slowly at first, and then less slowly, and then he understands she is hungry in the way a person is hungry who has been measuring her food for several days, and he gets up without comment and cuts another two slices of bread and puts them in the skillet with two more slices of cheese, and when they are done he slides the second sandwich onto her plate without asking.

She looks up at him.

"Thank you," she says.

"You're welcome."

She eats the second sandwich more slowly than the first.

Boaz is lying on the rag rug in front of the stove. He has his chin on his front paws and his eyes are closed and the firelight is moving on his fur in the way firelight moves, which is the oldest moving light there is, older than electricity by a hundred thousand years, and the dog has surrendered to it the way dogs surrender to the oldest things.

"What's your name?" Hank says, when she has finished.

"Ruth," she says.

"Ruth," he says. "Hank."

"Hank," she says.

She does not offer a last name. He does not ask.

She does, after a moment, ask him a question. Which, given the day she has had, is more than he had any right to expect.

"Whose cabin is this?" she says.

"Mine," he says. "It was my wife's father's. He built it. My wife and I came up here every summer for forty years and most Christmases. She passed in May."

Ruth nods, slowly, looking at the table again.

"I'm sorry," she says.

"Thank you."

"That's her crossword," Ruth says. "Isn't it."

Hank looks at the crossword between them. He has not touched it. He has been afraid to touch it, in a way he could not have explained even to Pastor David, who has known him for thirty-one years.

"Yes," he says. "It is."

Ruth reaches out, very carefully, and she straightens the pencil so that it lies parallel to the long edge of the puzzle. She does not move the puzzle. She does not move the glasses or the mug. She moves only the pencil, by an inch, so that it is straight.

Then she puts her hands back in her lap.

Hank sits across the table from her and he looks at the pencil where she has straightened it and he does not trust his voice for a moment.

He says, finally, "It's a fold-out couch. The couch. I'll get the sheets."

Twelve

He makes up the couch while she is in the bathroom again brushing her teeth. He has sheets in the chest at the foot of the bed in the bedroom — Eleanor's good flannel sheets, the ones with the pattern of small blue cornflowers, washed once and folded and put away in May before they came back down off the mountain for the last time. He had not, until tonight, known that he would be the one to take them out of the chest.

He shakes out the bottom sheet over the foldout mattress. The smell of cedar from the chest comes up off the sheet, and underneath the cedar, very faint, the smell of her laundry soap.

He fits the corners. He shakes out the top sheet. He puts down two pillows from the bedroom and a wool blanket from the chair, and he folds a quilt at the foot of the couch in case she gets cold in the night.

The quilt is one Eleanor made the second winter they were married, out of squares cut from his old work shirts. It is the most personal object in the cabin. He had not, when he reached for it, intended to put it on her bed. His hand reached for it without consulting him. He let his hand have its way.

He stands back. He looks at the made-up couch. It looks like a bed for a person.

He thinks, *There has not been a bed made up for a guest in this cabin since the summer before she got sick.*

He is standing there when Ruth comes back out of the bathroom. She has her hair tied back now in a loose knot at the base of her neck. She sees the bed. She sees the quilt folded at the foot of it. She does not say anything for a moment.

Then she says, "You didn't have to do all that."

"It's no trouble," he says.

"The dog can sleep with me," she says. "If that's all right. He shakes if he doesn't."

"It's all right," he says. "He's a good dog."

"He's the only one that came with me," she says. "Out of all of them."

Hank does not ask out of all of who. He does not need to. The sentence, by itself, contains a great deal.

He says, "There's a glass of water on the side table. The bathroom light has a switch by the door. The lock on the front door is the deadbolt. The key is on the hook."

"Thank you," she says.

"Goodnight, Ruth."

"Goodnight."

He goes to the bedroom. He shuts the door but not all the way — he leaves it open a hand's width, in case the dog needs water or in case she needs anything in the night — and he sits on the edge of the bed for a long time without taking off his boots.

He hears her turn off the lamp.

He hears the soft, careful sound of her getting under the blanket. He hears the quilt being shaken out, gently. He hears the dog jump up onto the foot of the couch and turn around once and lie down with a long, settling sigh.

Then he hears nothing for a long time.

Then, very faintly, through the open hand's width of the bedroom door, he hears the sound of a young woman crying. She is crying as quietly as a person can cry, with a hand over her mouth, into a pillow. He hears her for perhaps three minutes. Then he hears her stop. Then he hears her breathing slow down, and then he hears her breathing even out, and then she is asleep.

He sits on the edge of the bed in the dark and he does not move.

After a while, he gets up. He takes off his boots. He sets them by the door. He lies down on top of the bedspread, on his side of the bed, the side closer to the door, the side he has slept on for forty years. He puts his hand out across the bedspread to the place where, for forty years, his hand reached at night and found her.

There is nothing there. He had not, somehow, been prepared for there to be nothing there in this bed too.

He lies there a long time.

Outside, sometime after midnight, the rain becomes snow.

Thirteen

He wakes once, in the dark, to the sound of the wind. The wind has come around to the north and it is moving in the pines in the way the north wind moves in the pines, which is with intent. He hears a branch fall somewhere on the slope above the cabin. He hears it crack and ride and land.

He gets up. He goes to the bedroom window in his socks and he looks out.

The world has gone white.

Not deeply. Three inches, maybe four. But enough — enough to bend the pine boughs and to round the edges of the woodpile and to soften the truck where it sits beside the porch, the green of it turned the color of moonlight under the snow. The snow is still falling. It is falling straight down now, the wind having quieted, and it is falling thickly, the flakes the size of moths.

He stands at the window in his socks and he watches it fall.

He does not, at this hour, have words for what he feels. He will not have them in the morning either. There is something in him that recognizes, the way a body recognizes weather, that the road down the mountain will not be passable for at least a day, and there is something else in him, something he does not look at directly, that is glad of it.

He goes back to bed.

He sleeps.

He sleeps better than he has slept in six months and twelve days.

Fourteen

In the morning the sun comes up gold on the snow. It comes up over the Mingus range the way it has come up over the Mingus range every morning since the cabin was built, and the light slants in low through the kitchen window onto the floor and lies there in a long bar that contains, when he comes out into the great room and stops to look at it, every mote of dust in the cabin, lifting and turning slowly in the light.

The fire in the stove is down to coals. The dog is asleep on the rag rug. Ruth is asleep on the couch, on her side, one hand tucked up under her cheek, the quilt pulled up to her chin. Her face in sleep is younger than her face awake. He looks at her for one moment, no longer, and then he looks away, because looking at a sleeping woman who is not your wife is not a thing a man does, even at sixty-seven, even with no wife left to be unfaithful to.

He goes to the stove. He opens the door, quietly. He lays two more splits of pine on the coals. He shuts the door.

He goes to the kitchen window with the coffee pot in his hand and he stands there filling it from the tap and he looks out at the snow.

The pines are bent under it. The woodpile has a white roof. The truck has been swallowed up to the wheel wells. There is a ponderosa branch down across the bed of the truck — the one he heard fall in the night — a good-sized branch, eight or nine feet long, and he can see from here that it is going to take some moving.

He thinks, *That truck is not going anywhere today.*

He thinks, after a moment: *That girl is not going anywhere today either.*

He puts the coffee on.

He hears, behind him, the small sounds of someone waking up on a strange couch in a strange house. The shifting of the quilt. The dog's tail thumping once on the floor in greeting. The soft surprised breath of a person who is, for a moment, not sure where she is, and then, a moment later, remembers.

He does not turn around.

"Coffee," he says, to the kitchen window. "It'll be ready in a minute."

Behind him, quietly, she says, "I can see snow."

"Yes," he says. "We got some."

He turns around then. She is sitting up on the couch with the quilt around her shoulders like a shawl, and she is looking out the window over the back of the couch at the white world beyond it. Her hair has come partly out of its knot and is hanging on one side of her face, and her eyes are the brown of river stones in shallow water, and she is looking at the snow with the open face of a person who has not, in a long time, looked at anything with an open face.

"I haven't seen snow," she says, "in three years."

"Where've you been," he says, "that there hasn't been snow?"

"Albuquerque," she says. "South Valley."

He nods. He gets two mugs down from the cabinet.

"How do you take it?" he says.

"Black," she says. "Please."

"That's how I take it," he says.

He pours them both a cup. He carries hers over to the couch and hands it to her. She takes it in both hands, as a person takes a cup of coffee that is the first warm thing of the day, and she holds it under her chin and she lets the steam come up onto her face, and she closes her eyes for a second.

"Thank you," she says.

"You're welcome."

He sits down in the leather chair across from the couch with his own cup. The dog gets up off the rag rug and pads over and lays his chin on Hank's knee, uninvited. Hank, who has not had a dog in twenty years, looks down at the dog. The dog looks up at him with the patient, full-hearted look of a dog who has decided, on his own and without consultation, that this morning is going somewhere good.

Hank scratches him behind the ear.

Outside, in the pines, a branch lets go of its load of snow and the snow falls and is heard.

Inside, by the stove, the fire has caught the new pine and is going steady.

Two cups of coffee are steaming in two pairs of hands.

Nobody says anything for a long time.

It is, by Hank's count, the most peaceful five minutes he has had since the seventh of May.

Fifteen

He cooks them both eggs and bacon and the last of the bread, toasted, and they eat at the kitchen table with the crossword puzzle still between them and the pencil that Ruth straightened the night before still where she straightened it. She eats more slowly than she ate last night. She is not as hungry as she was. That, in itself, tells him something — that she had been hungry, last night, in a way she had not wanted to admit, and that one meal and one good night's sleep have gone some distance toward restoring her to herself.

She is twenty-four, she says, when he asks. She tells him a little, not much. She grew up in Albuquerque. Her mother is dead, six years now, of an aneurysm at forty-two — sudden, no warning, gone before the ambulance got there. Her father is in California with a woman who is not her mother and was not her mother before her mother died either, although Ruth does not put it quite that way. She has two younger half-brothers she has not seen since she was nineteen. She worked, until a month ago, in the kitchen of a breakfast place on Central Avenue, which is why she knows how to make biscuits, which is why she knows how to make a great many things, which is why he should not, she says with the smallest curve at one corner of her mouth, expect her to be useless around the kitchen for as long as she is here.

He asks her where she was going.

"Sedona," she says. "Maybe. I had a friend up there. I haven't talked to her in a year and a half. I thought she might still be there. I thought I would just — go."

"You walked," he says.

"I had a ride out of Albuquerque," she says. "As far as Flagstaff. And another ride down to Camp Verde. And then I walked. I'd been walking three days when you found me. I came up the wrong road. I was trying to get to Highway 89 and I missed the turn somewhere back of Mayer and I just kept going up. I thought if I kept going I'd hit something."

"You hit something," he says.

She looks at him over the rim of her coffee cup.

"Yes," she says. "I did."

He does not ask her what she was running from. He does not ask her why a young woman in a thin jacket, with a dog on a clothesline, was walking up a mountain road in November alone.

He has a guess. He keeps it to himself.

After breakfast they put on coats — he loans her one of Eleanor's, a heavy wool barn coat that hangs almost to her knees but that fits across the shoulders, more or less — and they go outside to look at the truck.

The branch on the truck is bigger than it looked from the window. It is going to have to be cut up before it can be moved. The snow is past their ankles and a soft, intermittent flake is still coming down out of a sky that has gone the color of pewter.

"I've got a chainsaw in the lean-to," Hank says. "I'll cut it up after lunch. The road won't be passable till tomorrow afternoon at the earliest. They don't plow up here. The sun has to do it."

Ruth nods. She is standing in the snow in Eleanor's coat with her hands in the pockets of it and her head tipped back, looking up at the pines. The snow has caught in the boughs and the light on the snow in the boughs is the kind of light that makes a person tip her head back and look up at it.

"It's beautiful," she says, very quietly, almost to herself.

"Yes," Hank says. "It is."

He looks at her looking up at the pines, and then he looks up at the pines himself, and for the first time since the morning of the seventh of May he sees the snow in the boughs the way Eleanor would have seen it, which is to say, as a gift — given freely, without occasion, by a hand he has spent six months refusing to name.

He does not name it now.

But he sees it.

That, by itself, is something.

Sixteen

After lunch he goes out to the lean-to and gets the chainsaw and the bar oil and the small jerry can of two-stroke mix, and he carries them around to the truck. The sun has come out. The snow is letting go of the pine boughs in soft, intermittent surrenders, plopping wetly down onto the ground in patches the size of dinner plates. The sky overhead is a clean, washed blue.

Ruth comes out behind him in Eleanor's coat and stands at the porch rail with a mug of coffee in her hands.

"Can I help?" she says.

"You can stand back about ten feet," he says. "Chainsaws don't have a sense of humor."

She nods. She sits down on the top step instead.

He fills the saw. He primes it. He sets it on the snow and pulls the cord, and on the third pull it catches and runs, and then he is in the small private world of a man with a chainsaw, where there are no other thoughts than the cut he is about to make and the cut after that, and the wood gives up its piney smell into the cold air, and the chips fly, and the branch begins to come apart.

He cuts it into rounds. He works the saw down the length of the limb in even, deliberate sections, the way a man cuts firewood when he knows he is going to be the one stacking it. The branch is good ponderosa, and ponderosa, dry, will heat a cabin in November like nothing else, and there is no sense, he thinks, in wasting it. He cuts and cuts. Ruth, on the porch step, watches him work the way a person watches another person doing something they are good at, which is to say with a kind of quiet, unjudging attention that he has not had directed at him in some time, and that he does not let himself notice he is enjoying.

When the branch is in twelve rounds on the snow, he kills the saw. The silence comes back in. The whole forest seems to have been holding its breath.

He carries the rounds, two at a time, to the splitting block beside the lean-to. Ruth gets up off the porch and, without asking, starts carrying them too — one at a time, on her hip, the way she would have carried a sack of flour out of a pantry — and he does not stop her, because he has the sense that being useful is, for her, a thing she needs more than she needs to be told to sit down.

He splits the rounds with a maul. He has split a great many rounds with this maul, and the maul has worn the inside of his right hand into a shape that fits the handle the way a key fits a lock. The wood comes apart cleanly. Each split shows the heart of the round, pale gold and smelling of resin, and he stacks the splits along the lean-to wall the way Eleanor's father taught him to stack splits forty-one years ago, bark side down, the long axis running with the wall.

It takes them forty minutes. By the time they are done, both of them are warm under their coats, and Ruth has unbuttoned hers, and there is a streak of pine sap on her right cheek that she does not know is there.

"You've got sap," he says, gesturing.

She rubs at her cheek. She gets it on her hand instead.

"Other side," he says. "Higher."

She gets it.

She is laughing, a little, at herself. It is the first time he has heard her laugh. Her laugh is the laugh of a person who, somewhere under the tiredness and the watchfulness, is twenty-four years old and has not entirely forgotten how to be twenty-four.

He looks away. He looks at the woodpile. He says, "You stacked it right. Most people put the bark side up."

"My grandfather had a stove," she says. "He taught me."

"Where," he says.

"Truth or Consequences," she says. "New Mexico. He's been dead since I was twelve."

"Sounds like he taught you well."

"He did," she says. She is looking at the woodpile too, now, with the small private smile of a person remembering a man she loved. "He used to say you stack a pile right and it'll heat you twice. Once when you split it and once when you burn it."

"That's a true thing," Hank says.

"Yeah," she says. "It is."

They stand there in the snow looking at the wood they have stacked together. The sun is moving down toward the western ridge of the draw. The shadows of the pines are getting long across the white ground. Somewhere up the slope, a Steller's jay is yelling about something.

"I'll start dinner," Ruth says, after a while. "If that's all right. I told you not to expect me to be useless."

"I remember," Hank says.

"What've we got?"

"Not much. There's flour. Bacon. Eggs. A little butter."

She nods, slowly, the way a kitchen person nods when she is doing inventory in her head.

"Biscuits," she says. "Bacon and eggs. Gravy if there's enough drippings. That all right with you?"

"That sounds all right with me," he says.

He does not tell her that it sounds, in fact, like the best thing anyone has offered to make him in six months and twelve days.

Seventeen

The biscuits are something to see.

She works at the kitchen counter with her sleeves pushed up to her elbows, and she does not measure the flour. She pours it from the tin into a chipped white mixing bowl by feel, the way Eleanor used to pour flour, and she cuts the cold butter into it with two knives crossed, the old way, which Hank has not seen anyone do in twenty years. She mixes the dough with three fingers of one hand. She does not overwork it. She rolls it out on the floured board with a wine bottle, because there is no rolling pin, and she cuts the biscuits with the rim of the WORLD'S OKAYEST GRANDMA mug, which she has, very carefully, washed first.

He sits at the kitchen table with his second cup of coffee and he watches her work.

She is concentrating. Her tongue is touching the corner of her upper lip in a way she does not know it is doing. Her hands move over the dough with a quick, sure, unconsidered grace, the grace of someone who has done a thing ten thousand times and no longer needs to think about the doing of it, and Hank, who built cabinets for forty years, recognizes the grace of a craftsman when he sees it. She is, in this small floured patch of countertop, in her element.

He thinks, *She has not been in her element in some time.*

He thinks, *That is what was wrong with her last night.*

The biscuits go into the oven. The bacon goes in the cast iron. She fries the bacon down to crisp and she pours off most of the drippings into a coffee can and she keeps just enough for gravy. She makes the gravy with flour and milk in the same skillet, scraping the brown bits up off the bottom with a wooden spoon, and the gravy thickens the way good gravy thickens, in a slow, unhurried surrender. The eggs go in last, in the bacon fat, and she does them over easy.

The biscuits come out the color of old gold.

She sets the table. She uses the everyday plates, the ones with the small blue rim that Eleanor's mother bought at a yard sale in Chino Valley in 1979. She lays the forks on the napkins.

She puts the butter on a saucer. She sets a biscuit on each plate, splits it open, and ladles the gravy over half of it. She lays two strips of bacon and an egg beside the biscuit. She does not ask him how he likes his eggs. She has guessed correctly, and the guess, in itself, is a small kindness.

She sits down across from him.

"Thank you," he says. He says it before she has picked up her fork.

She looks at him. She does not say *you're welcome*. She does something better. She lowers her head, just a fraction, and she closes her eyes for a moment, and her lips move very faintly, and then she opens her eyes and picks up her fork.

She has said grace.

She has said it silently, because she did not know whether he would want her to say it aloud, and because she did not know whether she herself could have managed it aloud, and because grace, in her experience, has not lately been a thing said aloud at any table she has sat at.

Hank sees it. He does not comment. He picks up his fork.

But he does, in a way he does not show on his face, take note. The narrator might tell you, if the narrator were inclined to break in here, that this is the second time this evening that Ruth has done something Hank was not asking her to do — straightened a pencil on a dead woman's crossword last night, said grace over a cabin supper tonight — and that on neither occasion did Ruth do the thing for Hank's benefit.

She did each thing for her own.

That, the narrator might say, is the difference.

The biscuits are the best biscuits he has eaten since 1986. He tells her so.

"My grandmother's recipe," she says. "From Truth or Consequences."

"Your grandfather had a stove and your grandmother made biscuits," Hank says. "You came up well."

She does not answer that one. She looks down at her plate and she eats her egg.

"Did you," he says, after a moment, gentler. "Come up well, I mean."

She thinks about it.

"For a while," she says, finally. "I came up well for a while."

She does not say more. He does not ask.

Outside, through the kitchen window, the dusk is coming on, and the snow on the woodpile is going blue in the early shadow, and somewhere in the pines the Steller's jay has stopped yelling and gone home for the night.

Eighteen

The fire is going in the wood stove and the dishes are washed and dried and put away, and Ruth is sitting in one of the leather chairs by the fireplace with her bare feet pulled up under her and a mug of tea in her hands, and Hank is sitting in the other chair with his own mug, and Boaz is asleep on the rag rug between them, and nobody has spoken in something like ten minutes.

It is, Hank thinks, the kind of silence that comes only when two people have eaten a good meal together, and it is the kind of silence Eleanor used to call *the easy kind*, to distinguish it from the other kind, which is the kind that means somebody has something to say and is not saying it.

He does not, tonight, have something to say.

He is, in fact, very nearly content. He is aware of the strangeness of this — that he should be very nearly content, in this cabin, on the seventeenth of November, six months and thirteen days after his wife has died, in the company of a young woman he did not know existed twenty-four hours ago. He examines the strangeness from a small distance, the way a man examines a piece of wood whose grain is running in an unexpected direction. He does not try to make it run any other way.

After a while Ruth says, into the fire, "Can I ask you something?"

"You can ask."

"Why is the cross turned around?"

He is, briefly, surprised. He had not been sure whether she had registered it, that first night, and he had not been sure, in the day and a half since, whether to bring it up. He considers, for a moment, several different answers. He chooses, in the end, the true one.

"Because I'm angry at God," he says. "And I haven't been able to look Him in the face for six months."

She nods. She does not say anything for a little while.

Then she says, "I haven't been inside a church in three years."

It is, in its own way, a reciprocal kindness — the trading of an honest thing for an honest thing.

"What happened?" he says.

She is quiet for a long moment. She is looking at the fire. The firelight is on her face and on the small silver cross at her throat and on the rim of the mug in her hands.

"There was a man," she says, finally. "At the church I grew up in. He was the youth pastor. He was thirty-eight and I was sixteen. He told me — for two years he told me — that what we had was a special thing that God had given us, and that I shouldn't talk about it, because the world wouldn't understand."

She pauses. She has not, he can tell, said any of this aloud to anyone in a long time, and saying it aloud is costing her something, and she is paying the cost with the steady, careful voice of a person who has already paid it many times before, in private, and knows the price.

"I believed him," she says. "I was sixteen. I believed him for two years."

She looks at the fire. She does not look at Hank.

"When I told my pastor — the senior pastor, the one over him — when I finally told him, when I was eighteen, the senior pastor said it was complicated. He said the youth pastor had a wife and three kids and a good ministry and he was sorry, he was so very sorry, but that we had to *think about the testimony of the church.* That was the phrase he used. *The testimony of the church.* And that I should pray about whether I had — "

She stops. She takes a breath.

" — whether I had contributed to the situation. Those were his words. *Contributed to the situation.*"

Hank does not say anything. He has, very gently, set his mug down on the side table, because his hand is not entirely steady, and he does not want her to see it tremble.

"My mother was already dead by then," Ruth says. "And my father was already gone. And the church — the church was the only family I had. So I left the church. And I have not been back inside one. And every time I see a cross, I think about that pastor's hand on my shoulder while he prayed for me. And every time someone tells me to *trust God*, I think about the senior pastor saying *the testimony of the church*."

She lifts the small silver cross at her throat in two fingers. She looks down at it.

"This was my mother's," she says. "I keep wearing it because she gave it to me. Not because I believe what it means anymore. I don't know what I believe anymore. I haven't known for three years."

She lets the cross fall back against her collarbone.

"I'm not telling you this so you'll fix it," she says. "I'm telling you because you turned that cross around. And I wanted you to know I understand."

The fire pops, once, in the stove. A small piece of pitch catches and flares and is gone.

Hank sits with his hands on his knees, and he looks across the rag rug at this twenty-four-year-old woman in a borrowed chair who has, in the space of two minutes, given him a piece of her life that no one in the world is probably entitled to, and he understands, with a clarity that is also a kind of grief, that he has been given something he does not deserve.

"Ruth," he says.

She looks at him.

"I'm going to tell you something," he says. "And I want you to know it before I say it: nothing that happened to you was your fault. Not one inch of it. The man who told you it was a special thing was a liar, and the man who told you to pray about your contribution was a liar, and any God who would back either of them up isn't a God I want anything to do with either."

She is looking at him. Her eyes are wet, but she is not crying. She is holding very still.

"And I'll tell you the other thing too," he says. "It is taking me a long time to figure out — and I have not figured it out yet, you understand, I am still working on it — but I think that God is not the same thing as the men who use His name. I think Eleanor would tell you that, if she were sitting where I am sitting. I cannot tell you that yet. Not with the conviction she could. But I think she would have. And I trusted her judgment in everything that mattered for forty years, so I am going to start by trusting it in this."

Ruth is, now, crying. Quietly. The tears are coming down her face one at a time, without sound, and she is not wiping them away.

"I'm sorry," she says.

"Don't be sorry."

"I haven't told anyone," she says. "I haven't told anyone in three years."

"I know," he says. "Thank you for telling me."

Boaz, sometime in the last minute, has gotten up off the rag rug and gone over to Ruth's chair and laid his chin on her knee. She puts her hand down on his head. She keeps her hand there.

The fire goes on burning.

Nobody says anything for a long time.

After a while, Hank gets up. He goes into the kitchen. He fills the kettle. He puts it on the gas burner. He gets two clean mugs down from the cabinet and he gets the box of teabags out of the cupboard, and he stands at the counter with his back to the great room while the kettle heats, and he gives her the privacy of the kettle's small rising sound.

When the kettle whistles he makes the tea. He carries both mugs back into the great room. He sets hers on the small table next to her chair.

"Mint," he says. "Eleanor liked it before bed."

"Thank you," she says. Her voice is steadier now.

He sits back down.

After a while she says, "Hank."

"Mm."

"What was she like?"

He thinks about how to answer. He thinks about it for a long time. The fire pops. Boaz sighs in his sleep on Ruth's foot.

"She was kinder than I deserved," he says, finally. "And smarter than she let on. She played the piano. Not well, but with her whole heart, which is the better of the two ways to play. She made coffee too strong. She remembered the names of every waitress in every diner we ever ate at twice. She believed in God the way some people believe in weather — not as a question, just as a fact that the day is built around. And she could finish my sentences before I had figured out what I was going to say in them."

He stops. He looks at the fire.

"I miss her," he says, "every minute of every day. And it has not gotten easier. People say it gets easier. It hasn't gotten easier. It has only gotten quieter. I think those are different things."

Ruth nods, slowly.

"That's why the cross is turned around," she says.

"That's why," he says.

They sit there a long time more.

The fire dies down. He gets up, eventually, and lays one more split on it, a smaller one, enough to last till morning, and he banks the coals along the back wall of the firebox.

"I should sleep," Ruth says.

"Yes."

He goes to the bedroom door. He stops with his hand on the frame.

"Ruth."

"Yes."

"Thank you for telling me. I mean it."

"Thank you for listening."

"Goodnight."

"Goodnight, Hank."

He goes into the bedroom. He shuts the door, again, to a hand's width.

He lies down on top of the bedspread, on his side. He looks at the dark ceiling. He thinks, *I have just heard something I will carry the rest of my life,* and he is not, this time, surprised that the thought has come to him in those words, because he has known, for some hours now, that this week is going to be a marker in his life in a way he had not, when he turned the truck around in the rain, anticipated it being.

He sleeps.

He sleeps lightly.

Nineteen

He wakes around two in the morning.

It is the small, specific waking of an old man who has, somewhere in his sleep, registered a sound that does not belong. He lies still in the dark, listening.

There is a sound. It is a small sound. It is the sound of pages turning, very slowly, very carefully, in the great room.

He gets up. He puts his feet down on the cold wood floor. He goes, in his socks, to the bedroom door. He opens it the rest of the way, slowly, so that the hinges do not speak.

The lamp on the side table by the leather chair is on. Ruth is sitting in the chair with her legs pulled up under her and the quilt around her shoulders. Boaz is asleep across her feet. She has a book open in her lap.

The book is Eleanor's Bible.

It is the brown leather one Eleanor kept by the chair, the one she read from every morning for the last twelve years of her life, the one with her small precise handwriting in the margins of nearly every page. Hank had not, in six months and thirteen days, brought himself to take it down from the shelf. It had been on the bookshelf above the stove when he came in two evenings ago, and it had been on the bookshelf above the stove this morning, and he had not, either time, looked directly at it.

Ruth has it open in her lap.

She is not reading. Or she is reading, but not the way one reads a book one is in a hurry to finish. She is turning a page. She is looking at it. She is turning another. He realizes, after a moment, what she is doing.

She is reading Eleanor's marginalia.

She is reading the small precise handwriting in the margins. She is reading, that is to say, not the text of the Bible itself but the conversation Eleanor was having with the text — the underlines, the question marks, the dates, the small notes that say things like *J.'s funeral, August '04* or *kept thinking about this on the drive home* or, in one place that Hank himself had read once and never been able to read again, *Ask H. about this.*

Ruth turns another page. She stops on it. She reads. Hank cannot see, from the bedroom door, what page it is. But he can see that she has stopped.

She puts her finger on the page.

She closes her eyes.

Her lips move, very faintly. She is not, he understands, reading aloud. She is reading silently, or she is praying silently, or she is doing the thing that is neither one and not quite the other but which lies in the space between the two, and which a person who has not been in a church in three years might find herself doing, alone, in a stranger's lamplight, in the small hours of a November morning, when a strange dog is asleep on her feet and a strange quilt is around her shoulders and a strange Bible is open on her lap to a page someone else loved before her.

Hank does not go in. He does not interrupt her.

He stands at the bedroom door in his socks for what is probably a full minute. Then he steps back, very quietly, into the bedroom. He does not close the door. He sits down on the edge of the bed. He puts his face in his hands.

He does not cry. He has still not cried since the funeral.

But something in him gives, a little, in a way that has not given before.

He does not know what to call it. He is, at sixty-seven, too old and too plain a man to have language for the thing happening in his chest. He thinks, vaguely, of a piece of dovetailed wood on a humid day – how the joint, after a long dry winter, draws back together when the moisture comes; how the wood remembers the shape it was supposed to be in, and finds its way back to it without anyone helping.

He sits on the edge of the bed for a long time.

In the great room, the soft sound of pages turning has stopped. Then, after a while, it starts again, slower than before. Then it stops. Then he hears the soft click of the lamp being turned off. Then he hears Ruth settle back down on the couch under the quilt, and the small adjusting of the dog, and then, at last, nothing.

He gets up. He goes to the bedroom window. He looks out.

The moon has come up over the ridge. It is a three-quarter moon, very white, and the snow under it is the color of new paper. The pines are black against the snow. Out beyond the truck, where the dirt road bends down out of the draw, he can see the silver line of it running away into the trees.

He stands there a long time.

He says, into the quiet of the room, very quietly, almost not aloud:

"All right."

That is all he says. He does not say to whom.

He goes back to bed.

This time he does not lie on top of the bedspread. He gets under the covers. He pulls them up to his chin. He closes his eyes.

He sleeps, the rest of that night, a deep and dreamless sleep, the kind he has not slept since the seventh of May.

In the great room the wood stove holds its coals against the cold. In the bookshelf above the stove, the place where Eleanor's Bible had sat for six months and thirteen days is empty. The Bible is on the side table next to the leather chair, closed now, with a folded paper bookmark — torn from a grocery list in Eleanor's handwriting

— marking a page in the middle of the eighty-fourth Psalm.

The page Ruth had stopped on.

The page that says, in Eleanor's small precise hand, in the margin beside the fifth verse:

Yes. Yes. This.

PART THREE

The Light in the Window

Twenty

He wakes to the sound of coffee.

The smell of it first — coffee being made by someone who knows how to make it, in a kitchen that is not his kitchen but is his cabin, and the smell is the smell of a morning that has begun without him, which is a thing he has not woken up to in six months and fourteen days.

He lies a moment in the bed with his eyes closed and he listens.

There is the soft clink of a spoon against a mug. There is the small particular sound of butter going into a hot skillet. There is, after a moment, the sound of a young woman humming, very softly, a tune he does not at first recognize — and then, slowly, from far back somewhere in his life, recognizes, the way a man recognizes the face of a person he met once at a wedding thirty years ago. *Be Thou My Vision*. She is humming it the way a person hums when she is not aware she is humming.

He gets up. He puts on his pants and his flannel shirt and his socks. He runs his hand through his hair. He goes out into the great room.

The fire is up in the wood stove. The blinds are open. The morning light is coming through the kitchen window in the same long bar it came through yesterday and the day before, except that today the bar of light has someone standing in it.

Ruth is at the stove with her back to him. She is making something in the cast iron. Her hair is in a single braid down her back. She has Eleanor's barn coat hung on the back of a kitchen chair within easy reach, the way a person hangs a coat she expects to put on within the hour.

He understands, before she has turned around, that this is the morning she leaves.

"Morning," he says.

She turns. She has flour on the bridge of her nose. She has, this morning, the steady, settled face of a person who has slept all the way through and woken up rested, and there is something else in her face he has not seen there before, something that, if he had to put a word on it, he might call *clear*.

"Morning," she says. "I'm making the last of the biscuit dough. There's coffee."

"I see that."

"I figured I should put the flour in the tin to use before you closed the cabin up."

"That was a kind thought."

"It was a selfish thought," she says, with a small private smile. "I wanted biscuits."

He pours himself a cup of coffee. He sits down at the kitchen table. The crossword puzzle is still there. The pencil is where Ruth straightened it on the first night. The reading glasses. The mug.

He notices, this morning, that he can look at them without his throat closing.

He notices it. He sets it aside to think about later. He looks instead at Ruth, standing in the bar of morning light at the stove of the cabin Eleanor's father built, in Eleanor's barn coat, with flour on her nose, humming *Be Thou My Vision,* on what is, by his count, the eighteenth of November, a Wednesday, in the sixty-seventh year of his life and the third year, by her count, that she has not been inside a church.

He thinks, *I will remember this morning until the day I die.*

He sets that thought aside too.

"The road clear?" he says.

"I checked at first light," she says. "Sun's been on it since dawn. It's mud now, not snow. You could drive a truck on it if the truck had four-wheel drive."

"My truck has four-wheel drive."

"I figured it would."

She slides the biscuits onto a plate. She brings the plate to the table. She sits down across from him with her own coffee.

They eat without talking for a while. Boaz has his chin on Hank's foot under the table. The dog has, sometime in the last forty hours, decided that Hank is part of his world now, and Hank has, in the same span of time, decided the same thing about the dog without consulting himself on the matter.

"Where will you go," Hank says, after a while.

She looks at her coffee.

"I don't know yet," she says. "I was going to say Sedona. But I don't think I'm going to Sedona."

"No?"

"The friend up there — I haven't talked to her in a year and a half. I think I was using her like a — like a place to be going. I don't think she's actually where I'm going."

He nods.

"I think I might go home," she says.

"Albuquerque."

"Yes. There's a — there was a woman at the breakfast place where I worked. She kept asking me to come to her church. A different church. A small one. She wasn't pushy about it, she just kept asking. I told her no for a year. I think I might tell her yes now. I think I might call her when I get back."

"That sounds all right," Hank says.

"It might be a mistake," Ruth says. "I might walk in the door and walk right back out. I don't know yet. But I think I want to find out."

"That sounds like a good way to find out."

"Yeah," she says. "I think so too."

She eats half of her second biscuit. She sets the other half down on her plate.

"Hank," she says.

"Mm."

"I want to give you something. Before I go."

He waits.

She reaches up to the back of her neck, under her braid, and she works the small clasp of the chain at her throat. The chain comes free in her hand. She lays it on the table between them, the small silver cross at the end of it, the one her mother gave her before her mother died, the one she has been wearing for six years without believing what it meant.

She slides it across the table to him.

"I don't want you to keep it," she says. "I want you to hold onto it for me. Until I — until I know what I think it means again. I'd rather it be here, in this cabin, on a nail or in a drawer somewhere, than around my neck while I figure that out. Because I don't want to wear it the wrong way again. I wore it the wrong way for three years and I don't want to do that again."

Hank looks at the small silver cross on the table between them.

He picks it up. The chain pools into his palm. The cross is no bigger than the nail of his little finger, and it is warm from her skin.

"I'll hold it for you," he says.

"Thank you."

"Ruth."

"Yes."

"I'd like to give you something too. Wait here a minute."

He gets up. He goes to the side table by the leather chair, where Ruth left Eleanor's Bible the night before, closed, with the folded grocery-list bookmark in the eighty-fourth Psalm. He picks the Bible up. He carries it back to the table. He sets it down in front of her.

She looks at it.

"Hank," she says. "I can't take that. That's hers."

"It is," he says. "And she would have wanted you to have it. I am as sure of that as I have been of anything in six months. You read it last night, didn't you."

She looks at him. She does not, for a moment, answer.

"I came out for water," he says. "I saw the lamp. I went back to bed. I didn't want to interrupt you. The bookmark is in a different place this morning than it was when she put it in there."

She nods, slowly.

"I read some," she says. "Yes."

"Take it home with you," he says. "Read the rest of it. Read the parts she wrote in the margins. You'll know her better by reading her handwriting on those pages than you would have known her by sitting across a table from her. She put forty years of herself into those margins. Take it. Please."

She looks at the Bible on the table. She puts her hand on the cover. Her hand stays there for a long moment.

"All right," she says, very quietly. "All right."

She picks it up. She holds it against her chest with both hands, the way a person holds a thing she has been given that is more valuable than she can explain.

"Thank you," she says.

"Don't thank me," Hank says. "Thank her."

"I will," Ruth says. "I think I have been already, actually. Last night."

He nods.

He cannot, for the moment, trust his voice.

Twenty-One

He drives her down to the Greyhound station in Prescott Valley. He had offered to drive her all the way to Albuquerque, but she had said no, gently, that this was something she needed to do on her own legs from here, and he had understood, and he had not pressed her.

The drive down off the mountain is quiet. The morning sun is out and the snow is going fast off the south slopes and the dirt road is mud, the way she said it would be, but the truck is in four-wheel drive and the truck does not mind. Boaz is on the seat between them. Ruth has her hand on the dog's shoulder for the entire drive.

In Prescott Valley, at the station, he buys her ticket. She lets him. She does not, this morning, fight him about it.

"It leaves at twelve-forty," the woman at the counter says. "Boards at twelve-thirty. Dog rides for free if he stays in his crate."

"He'll stay in his crate," Ruth says.

They stand outside on the sidewalk for the half hour. They do not say much. There is not much that needs saying. He has bought her a sandwich at a gas station for the bus, and a bottle of water, and she has the Bible in the top of her pack, wrapped in the spare flannel shirt, where it will not get jostled.

When the driver opens the doors and starts loading bags, she turns to him.

"Hank."

"Ruth."

She does not hug him. He had not, somehow, expected her to. She is not, he understands, a person for whom physical affection comes easily, and he is not surprised to find that he is the same way, and he is glad that the morning has not asked it of either of them.

She puts her hand on his forearm instead. She squeezes once, hard. She lets go.

"Take care of yourself," she says.

"You too."

"Tell Pastor David I said thank you. For — for the casseroles. The ones he brought you, that you told me about. Tell him a stranger said thank you on his behalf."

"I will."

"And Hank."

"Yes."

She has her hand on the strap of her pack, ready to lift it. She looks at him directly for what might be the first time since she got into his truck three nights ago.

"You're going to be all right," she says. "You don't think you are. But you are."

He cannot, again, trust his voice. He nods.

"And so are you," he says, when he can. "I think so too."

She gets on the bus. The driver shuts the doors. Hank stands on the sidewalk and watches the bus pull out of the lot and turn east onto Highway 69, and the back of the bus gets smaller, and then he cannot see it anymore.

He stands there a minute longer, with his hands in the pockets of his coat.

Boaz is in the cab of the truck. Ruth had asked him to keep the dog. *He's safer with you,* she had said. *I'll be on a bus and then sleeping on a friend's floor for a while. He's been sleeping on dirt for two weeks. He needs a porch.* Hank had said yes without thinking about it, and it was only now, standing on the sidewalk in front of the Greyhound station in Prescott Valley with his old truck in the lot and a strange dog in the cab of it, that the size of what had happened began to register.

He had come up the mountain a man who was about to sell a cabin and shut a door. He was driving back up it with a dog he had not had three days ago and a small silver cross in his shirt pocket and a different kind of ache in his chest than the ache he had brought with him, and the cabin, for the first time in six months and fourteen days, was a place he wanted to be in rather than a place he wanted to be done with.

He went back to the truck. He got in. Boaz looked at him.

"I know," Hank said. "I miss her too."

He drove back up the mountain.

Twenty-Two

Pastor David Owen comes by that afternoon, around three.

He had called the day before, while Hank was outside cutting up the branch on the truck, and Ruth had answered the phone — Hank had told her to, in case it was Pastor David, and to tell him Hank was outside but that everyone was all right — and Pastor David had been so surprised by the unexpected female voice on the other end of the line that he had, by his own later admission, said *hello* three times before he had fully understood that he was being told that Hank was alive and well and would call him back later, and that the woman speaking to him was named Ruth and was a guest and was fine.

He had, in his own quiet way, made a mental note.

Now he is at the door, in his old fleece jacket and his work boots and a knit cap, with a casserole dish in his hands and Mrs. Owen's lasagna under the foil. He is fifty-six years old.

He is a small, plain, easy man with a face that has spent thirty years patiently absorbing other people's worst news, and the absorbing has worn itself into the lines around his eyes in a way that is gentle rather than tired. He has known Hank Marshall for thirty-one years and he buried Hank's wife in May.

"David," Hank says, opening the door.

"Hank."

"Come in. The dog will lick you."

"That's all right. I like dogs."

He comes in. Boaz licks him. He sets the lasagna on the kitchen counter. He looks around the cabin, slowly, the way a man looks around a room he has been in many times before, looking for the small differences.

He sees the fire going in the wood stove. He sees the dishes drying on the rack — two plates, two mugs. He sees the made-up couch. He sees, on the side table by the leather chair, the small folded square of paper that Hank has set there next to Eleanor's reading lamp — a torn piece of grocery list in Eleanor's handwriting, with nothing on it but the words *yogurt, oranges, wax paper*.

He sees, above the mantle, the wooden cross.

The cross is hanging the right way around again.

David looks at it. He does not say anything about it. He sits down in one of the leather chairs by the fireplace. Hank brings him a cup of coffee. Hank sits down in the other chair.

For a while, they sit.

"I called yesterday," David says.

"I know."

"A young woman answered the phone."

"Her name is Ruth," Hank says. "She's twenty-four. She was walking up the mountain in the rain three nights ago with a hurt dog and a thin jacket. The dog you just met. She slept on the couch for two nights. I just put her on the Greyhound to Albuquerque this morning."

David nods, slowly.

"That's a good thing you did," he says.

"She did me more good than I did her."

David does not say anything to that. He drinks his coffee.

After a while, Hank says, "She said to tell you thank you. For the casseroles. The ones you brought after Eleanor died. She said to tell you a stranger said thank you on your behalf."

David looks down at his coffee. He blinks twice, slowly.

"Tell her she's welcome," he says. "If you talk to her again."

"I'll tell her."

The fire pops in the stove. Boaz has gone back to the rag rug and is asleep with one paw twitching in some small dog dream.

"David," Hank says.

"Yes."

"I want to come back to church on Sunday."

David, who has been waiting six months and fourteen days for this sentence and has spent a not insignificant portion of that time praying for it without telling anyone he was praying for it, does not allow his face to do any of the things it might, in another man, have been excused for doing. He nods. He takes a drink of his coffee.

"All right, Hank," he says. "We'll save you a seat."

"I might not be much good at it for a while. I don't know what I think yet about — about a lot of it. I'm angry still. I haven't worked it out."

"Coming back angry is allowed," David says. "Coming back angry is, actually, how most people come back."

"Is that right."

"That is right. The ones who come back peaceful weren't gone in the first place. They just took a vacation."

Hank almost smiles. The almost-smile, which has been making more frequent appearances over the last seventy-two hours, makes another one now.

"What changed your mind?" David says, gently.

Hank thinks about how to answer.

He looks at the cross above the mantle. He looks at the rag rug where Boaz is asleep. He looks at the side table where the folded grocery list sits next to Eleanor's reading lamp, and in the drawer of which, he has put for the moment, a small silver cross on a fine silver chain, until he can decide where to keep it more permanently.

He looks at David.

"A girl in a thin jacket," he says.

David waits.

"And the eighty-fourth Psalm," Hank says. "And a quilt I made up with my own hands on a couch I didn't expect to be making up for anybody. And the way Eleanor used to make biscuits, and the fact that someone else still makes them that way somewhere in the world. And — "

He stops. He looks at his hands.

"And Eleanor," he says. "She wrote things in the margins of her Bible, David. Did you know that? She wrote in the margins her whole life. I hadn't been able to read them. I couldn't even take the Bible down off the shelf. The girl I told you about — she took it down. She read them in the middle of the night. While I was watching from the bedroom door without her knowing. And I — David, I don't know what to call what happened to me, watching her read my wife's handwriting in a book I'd been afraid of. But something — something put itself back together. I can't explain it any better than that. I'm a finish carpenter. I don't have the language for this."

David, who has spent thirty years among people who do not have the language for it, smiles a small and patient smile.

"You have the language for it just fine," he says. "Anybody who tells you you need fancier words than that is selling you something."

Hank laughs. It is a short laugh, and it surprises him, but it is a laugh.

David finishes his coffee. He sets the mug down on the side table.

"Sunday at ten," he says. "We'll save you a seat in the back if that's where you want to sit. Mrs. Owen will cry when she sees you. I'm telling you in advance. There is nothing I can do about it."

"That's all right," Hank says. "Tell her to bring tissues."

"I will."

David stands. He puts his hand on Hank's shoulder for a moment, the way he does, the way he has done for thirty-one years, and then he lets go and crosses to the door.

At the door he stops. He turns around.

"Hank."

"Yes."

"Eleanor used to tell me, every summer up here, that she didn't see why anyone needed a building to find God when there was this whole mountain. She said God built it before He built any of our churches. I used to argue with her about it. I used to say *come on, Ellie, the Body of Christ is the people, not the pines.* And she used to say, *David, why can't it be both.*"

He smiles.

"She was right, of course," he says. "She generally was. About most things. I'm just letting you know that if you ever feel like coming back to church is more church than you can manage on a given Sunday, this cabin counts. As far as I'm concerned. As far as I think she's concerned, too."

"David — "

"I'm leaving. I just wanted to say it. Sunday at ten."

He goes out. He shuts the door. Hank hears the truck start up in the drive. He hears it pull away down the mountain.

He sits in the leather chair for a long time.

Twenty-Three

Late afternoon, the light starting to go.

He puts on his coat. He whistles for the dog. The dog comes.

They walk out together along the dirt road, the mud freezing now in the long shadows where the sun has not been, the south slopes still bare and brown and warming. The pines are quiet. A nuthatch is working the bark of a ponderosa upside down, the way nuthatches do, undeterred by gravity, undeterred by anything. Somewhere far off, down the draw, a raven calls once and is answered.

Hank walks slowly. He has, he realizes, no particular destination. He is walking the way a man walks when he is not in a hurry to be anywhere, which is a way he has not walked, on this mountain or any other, in some time.

Boaz keeps pace beside him. The limp is almost gone. It will be gone, he thinks, in another day or two. The dog had needed only what most living things mostly need: a warm place out of the weather, and to be fed, and to be allowed to sleep next to another heartbeat.

It is possible, he thinks, that he had needed those things too.

He walks down to the bend in the creek where, yesterday, he and Ruth had stood together, and he stands there a moment looking at the water. The water is high with snowmelt. The water in the creek, at this bend, makes a sound like a woman laughing, very quietly, into her hand. Eleanor used to say so. Eleanor used to make him stop and listen to it on every walk they ever took down to this bend, for forty years.

He listens.

The water laughs.

He stands there a long time. He thinks about a great many things, and he thinks about nothing in particular, and the two activities, as Eleanor would have said, are not as distinct as people pretend.

The light is going gold, then pink, then the deep blue of high-country dusk in November.

He turns. He whistles. The dog comes.

They walk back up the road to the cabin together.

Twenty-Four

He builds a fire in the fireplace that night, not just in the wood stove but in the open stone fireplace too, which he has not built a fire in since the Christmas before Eleanor got sick. He sits in the leather chair with the firelight on his face. He has Eleanor's reading lamp on, on the side table, with nothing under it now to read. The Bible is gone. It is on a Greyhound somewhere east of Holbrook, at the moment, in the top of a young woman's hiking pack, wrapped in a flannel shirt.

He thinks of her on the bus. He thinks of the woman from the breakfast place she is going to call. He thinks of the small church she might walk into and might walk right back out of, and might not. He prays for her. He says nothing aloud. He just prays.

It is the first prayer he has prayed on purpose in six months and fourteen days, and it surprises him by being shorter than he would have expected, and gentler.

It says: *Take care of her. She has been by herself too long.*

That is the whole of it.

He sits with the dog at his feet and he watches the fire.

Outside, the mountain is dark. The cabin window, the one on the east side that faces the dirt road, has a single lamp burning in it, the small lamp on the side table next to the leather chair. The light it makes is not very large. It is just enough light to show, to anyone passing on the road below — a deer crossing the draw, a hawk in late flight, a stranger walking up the mountain in the rain looking for somewhere to come in out of the weather — that someone is home in this cabin tonight, and that the door is not locked against them.

It is enough light for that.

It is, in November, on a mountain, in the high country of Yavapai County, late on thc eighteenth of two thousand and twenty-four, all the light a window needs to give.

Twenty-Five

A letter comes to Hank Marshall in early March.

It comes to his house in Phoenix, which is where he has gone for the winter, the cabin shut up and waiting for the spring. The letter is in a plain white envelope with an Albuquerque return address he does not recognize. The handwriting on the front is small and precise and a little impatient, leaning forward into the next letter.

He stands in his front yard with the letter in his hand for a long moment before he opens it. He has had a kind of feeling about it from the moment he saw it in the mail.

He goes inside. He sits down at the kitchen table. He opens it.

Hank,

I have been meaning to write you for three months and I have not known how to start, so I am just going to start.

I went home. I called the woman from the breakfast place. Her name is Carmen. I went to her church the first Sunday in December. It is in a strip mall on Bridge Boulevard, between a tax preparer and a place that sells used appliances. There are about forty people on a good Sunday. The pastor is a woman about sixty-five years old who used to be a nurse. The first Sunday I went, I sat in the back row and I cried for the entire service, including the announcements, and Carmen sat next to me and held my hand and did not say a word about it. That is the kind of church it is.

I have been every Sunday since.

I am working at a bakery now, on Central, two blocks from where I used to work. The owner is teaching me to make sourdough. My hands are happy.

I read your wife's Bible most mornings, with my coffee, before my shift. I read the parts she wrote in. I am getting to know her. I think she would have liked me, Hank. I think we would have gotten on. I want you to know that I am taking very good care of it. The pages with her handwriting are the most underlined parts. I would have underlined the same parts. We seem to have agreed on what was important.

I want to give it back to you in the spring, if that is all right. Not because I don't want it. I am giving it back because I think I am ready to read a Bible of my own, and because I think Eleanor's belongs in the cabin where she read it. I would like to bring it to you in person. With Boaz, if that is all right too. I miss him every day. I will be a guest only. I will sleep on the couch and stay one night and I will not impose. I am asking, not telling.

The cross you are holding for me — I am not ready for it back yet. Hold on to it a little longer. I will know when it is time.

Tell Pastor David I think about him sometimes. Tell him my pastor's name is Pastor Inez and that I think he and she would like each other. Tell him she swears more than he probably does. He will laugh.

I am all right, Hank. I wanted you to know. You said I would be, and you were right, and I want to say it out loud to the one person who said it to me first.

Thank you for the soup. Thank you for the biscuits I made you. Thank you for the bed. Thank you for turning the truck around.

Yours, Ruth

He reads the letter twice.

He sits at the kitchen table for a long time after the second reading, with the letter in front of him and the envelope beside it.

Then he gets up. He goes to the kitchen counter where the calendar hangs, the one with the photograph of the Bradshaw Mountains on it that the volunteer fire department sells every year, and he turns it forward to May. He looks at the page. May is, in this calendar, a photograph of the Granite Dells at sunrise.

He picks up a pencil. He writes, in the square that is the second Saturday in May, three words.

Open the cabin.

He writes, beneath them:

Ruth coming.

He puts the pencil down.

He goes out into the back yard, where the bougainvillea is starting to come back, and he stands in the desert sun, and he closes his eyes.

The wind is moving in the palo verde out by the back fence. It is moving in a small, friendly way, the way the wind moves in a desert tree in Phoenix in early March, which is not the way the wind moves in a ponderosa in Yavapai County. But it is moving.

He listens to it.

He says, aloud, to nobody, to everybody, to the wind in the palo verde, to the God he is still working things out with, and to the wife who would, he knows now, have known how to make this prayer better than he can:

"Thank you."

That is the whole of it.

That is enough.

— *END* —

www.ingramcontent.com/pod-product-compliance
Lightning Source LLC
LaVergne TN
LVHW011029110826
845149LV00015B/3352

9781964172606